Originally published as *il destino di ACHILLE*
© 2009 edizioni ARKA, Milan
All rights reserved
www.arkaedizioni.it

First published in the United States of America in 2011 by
The J. Paul Getty Museum, Los Angeles

Getty Publications
1200 Getty Center Drive, Suite 500
Los Angeles, California 90049–1682

www.gettypublications.org

Whitney Braun, *Editor*
Pamela Heath, *Production Coordinator*

Printed by Stampe Violato, Bagnoli di Sopra, Italy (11C0066)
Bound by IGF, Aldeno (TN), Italy
First printing by the J. Paul Getty Museum (13031)

Library of Congress Control number: 2011924979

The Fate of
ACHILLES

Text inspired by Homer's *Iliad*
and other stories of ancient Greece

Text and illustrations by Bimba Landmann

The J. Paul Getty Museum
Los Angeles

But let us begin at the beginning.
Achilles is not yet born.
He is only a dream,
a thought as yet unformed
in his mother's heart.

Three gods divide power between them.
Zeus reigns over the vast heavens.
His brother Poseidon rules the foaming seas.
Their brother Hades is lord of the underworld.
This division creates perfect equilibrium.

Yet something, perhaps, is about to change.
One night, through the shining waters,
Zeus and Poseidon see the goddess Thetis,
daughter of the sea,
swimming like a silver fish.
She is wonderfully beautiful.
Zeus and Poseidon both fall madly in love.

The passion of an immortal is more furious than an earthquake.
If Zeus and Poseidon fight for her,
a dreadful battle will shake the world.

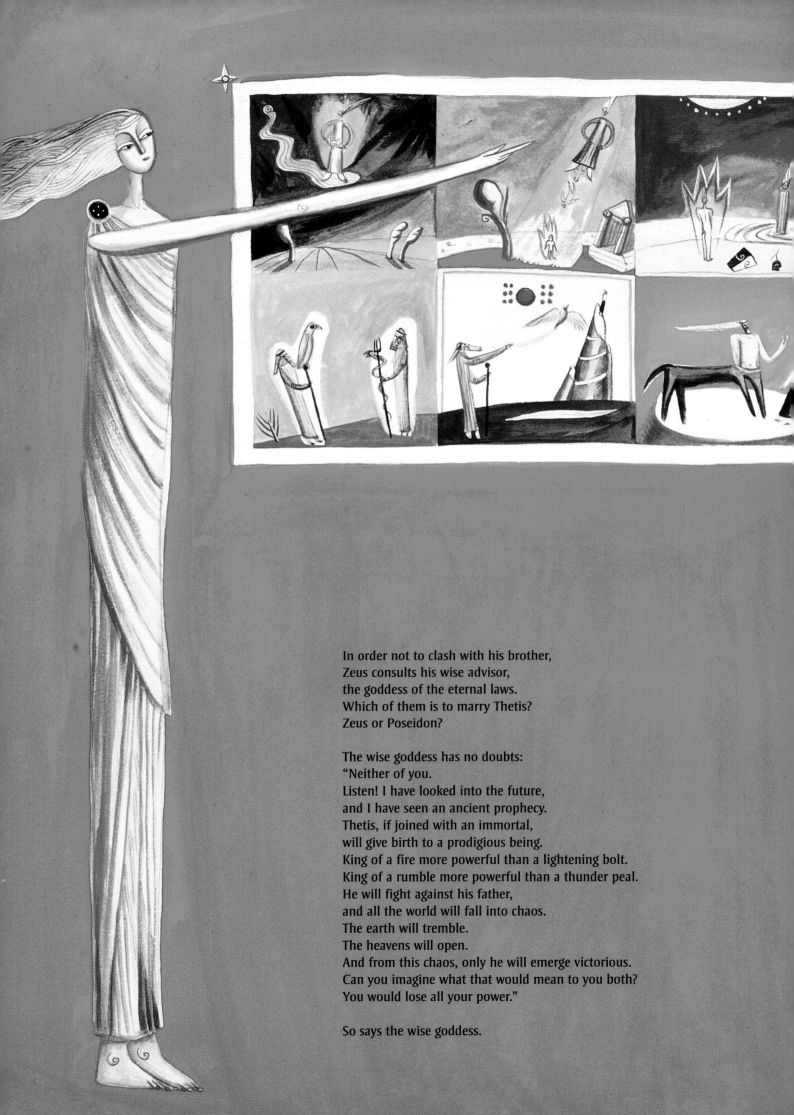

In order not to clash with his brother,
Zeus consults his wise advisor,
the goddess of the eternal laws.
Which of them is to marry Thetis?
Zeus or Poseidon?

The wise goddess has no doubts:
"Neither of you.
Listen! I have looked into the future,
and I have seen an ancient prophecy.
Thetis, if joined with an immortal,
will give birth to a prodigious being.
King of a fire more powerful than a lightening bolt.
King of a rumble more powerful than a thunder peal.
He will fight against his father,
and all the world will fall into chaos.
The earth will tremble.
The heavens will open.
And from this chaos, only he will emerge victorious.
Can you imagine what that would mean to you both?
You would lose all your power."

So says the wise goddess.

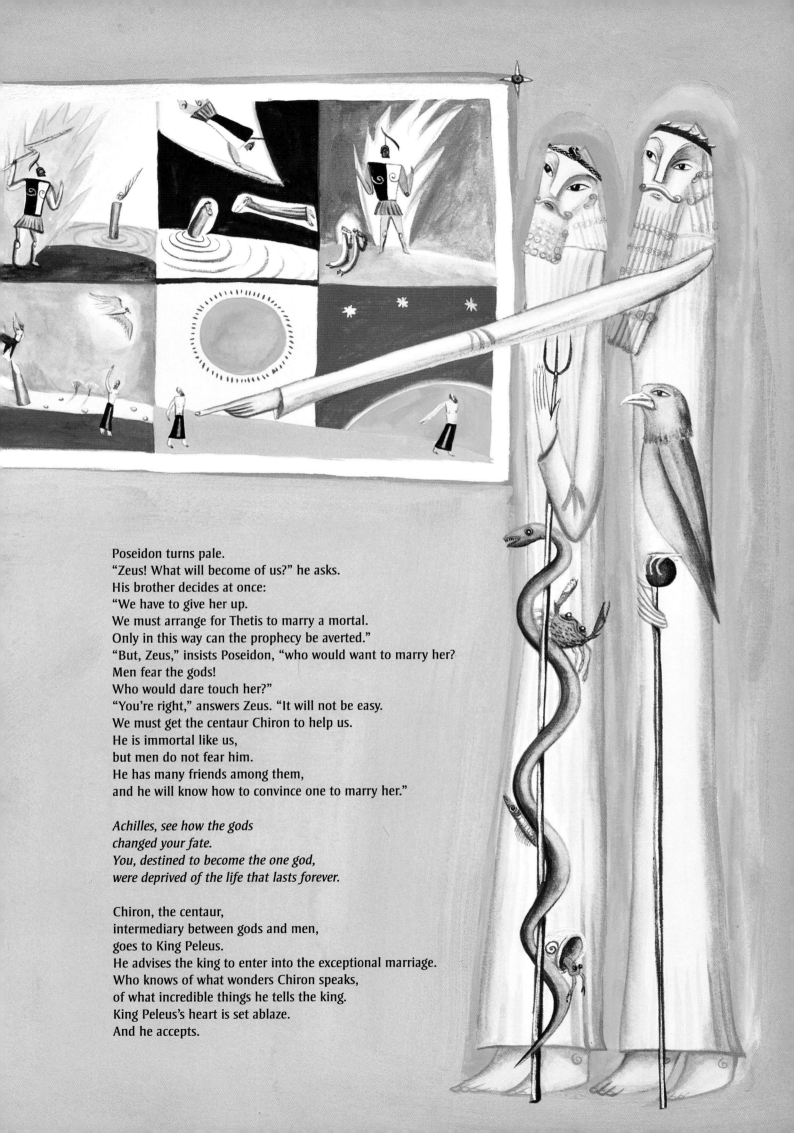

Poseidon turns pale.
"Zeus! What will become of us?" he asks.
His brother decides at once:
"We have to give her up.
We must arrange for Thetis to marry a mortal.
Only in this way can the prophecy be averted."
"But, Zeus," insists Poseidon, "who would want to marry her?
Men fear the gods!
Who would dare touch her?"
"You're right," answers Zeus. "It will not be easy.
We must get the centaur Chiron to help us.
He is immortal like us,
but men do not fear him.
He has many friends among them,
and he will know how to convince one to marry her."

Achilles, see how the gods
changed your fate.
You, destined to become the one god,
were deprived of the life that lasts forever.

Chiron, the centaur,
intermediary between gods and men,
goes to King Peleus.
He advises the king to enter into the exceptional marriage.
Who knows of what wonders Chiron speaks,
of what incredible things he tells the king.
King Peleus's heart is set ablaze.
And he accepts.

King Peleus listens as Chiron tells him the details.
"On the night of the next full moon," Chiron says,
"Thetis will be at the beach of the cuttlefish.
Catch her and hold her tight. It will not be easy.
She will try to escape with all her might. Stay calm.
And hold on to her *whatever happens*."

Whatever happens . . . Chiron had said.
But what Peleus now sees exceeds imagination.
As soon as he tries to embrace Thetis, she rebels.
She transforms into a living flame.
Then she turns to water.
Then a snake.
Lastly she becomes a cuttlefish.
Only then does Peleus dare caress her.
"There now," he says.
He feels the goddess settling down.
He feels her gradually becoming gentle.
And when she is once more a goddess and a woman,
Peleus loves her.

All the gods descend from Olympus
to celebrate the wedding
of Peleus and Thetis.
Even Ares, Demeter, and Apollo.
But why all this splendor?
Perhaps the gods already know
that from this marriage
a great hero will be born?
Yet a hero not great enough
to steal their power . . .

And on this day the Fates,
the goddesses who decide
the destinies of mortals,
give to the child who will be born
of this marriage a new destiny.

Achilles is still
in his mother's womb
when he hears
their obscure song:
*"Your fate is forever
tied to Troy.
No one can
undo this
knot."*

The hour of Achilles's birth
has come.
Like a tide,
the waves of childbirth
begin to rise
in Thetis's womb.
She immerses herself
in the ocean
and swims to the bottom
of the abyss.
There, she hides.

Thetis listens
to her womb contract.
Again and again.
She listens
as her secret, salty waters
flow into the secret,
salty waters
of the sea.

Then darkness
enfolds her
like a sheet.
And Achilles
comes into
the world.

But as Thetis holds her son tightly,
a pain strikes her heart
as sharply as a knife.
Her son will die,
for he is also the son of a mortal.

Immediately she flees the sea and hastens to the Styx,
the icy river of the underworld
that flows beneath the earth's crust.
The most pure of waters. The most magic of waters.
They make those who bathe in them invulnerable.
Thetis immerses Achilles in them.

Achilles, can a man really escape death?
Your mother's hand trembles.
Just for a moment.
And your heel remains dry.

Achilles is not rocked in the arms of Thetis.
She belongs to the sea, and to the sea she must return.
Peleus entrusts him to Chiron, the wise centaur.
"Train him as a warrior. Look after him."

Achilles is not brought up on mother's milk.
For him there must be food that gives strength.
Lion heart. Bear marrow. Boar liver.
But golden honey too, which gives sweetness.
Then Chiron begins to instruct him.
Achilles learns to hunt at seven.
At ten, he can tame a horse,
and fight with the sword,
and with the lance and his fists.

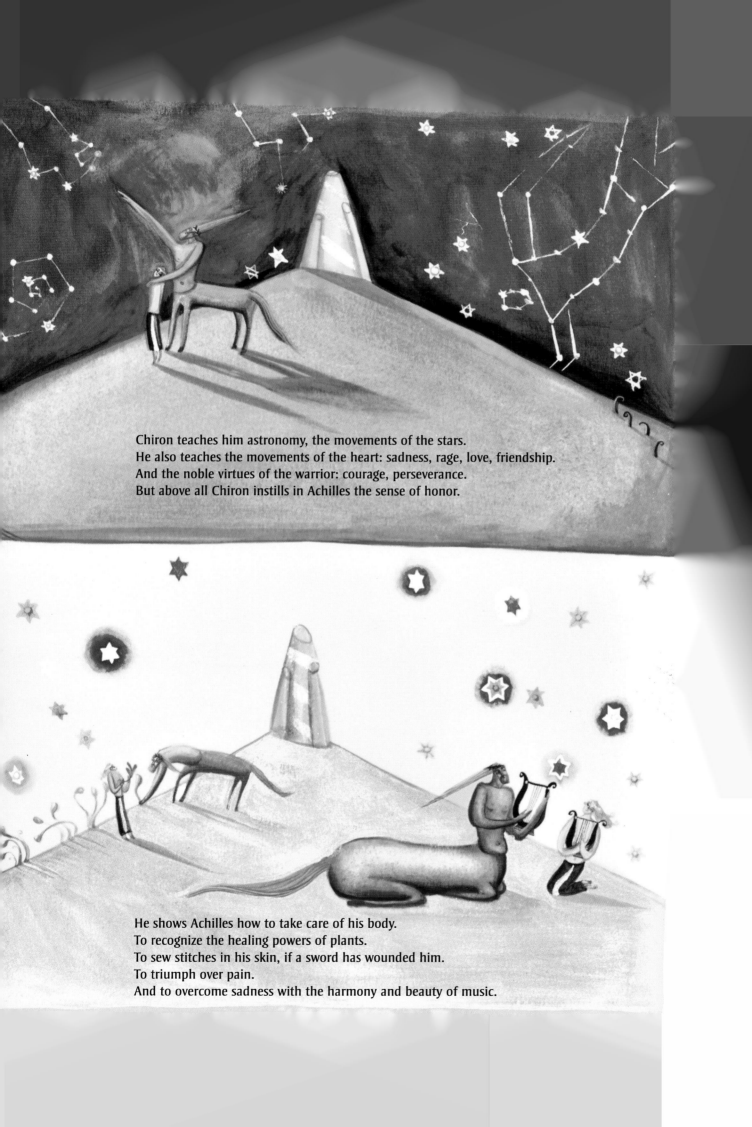

Chiron teaches him astronomy, the movements of the stars.
He also teaches the movements of the heart: sadness, rage, love, friendship.
And the noble virtues of the warrior: courage, perseverance.
But above all Chiron instills in Achilles the sense of honor.

He shows Achilles how to take care of his body.
To recognize the healing powers of plants.
To sew stitches in his skin, if a sword has wounded him.
To triumph over pain.
And to overcome sadness with the harmony and beauty of music.

Shaped by wisdom and strength,
Achilles feels rise within him
the desire to achieve noble feats.

And then, one day,
the great Ulysses comes to see him.
"King Agamemnon," Ulysses says, "is gathering an enormous army.
He will declare war on the Trojans, who have offended him
by abducting Helen, his brother's wife.
Achilles, join us in the fight. Help us to defend the honor of the Achaeans.
You are the son of a goddess: no one can match your strength!"
Ulysses is clever. He flatters Achilles. He must have Achilles on his side.
He has learned from the soothsayer Calchas
that Troy cannot be won without Achilles.

As Achilles loads his armor onto the warship, Thetis appears before him.
She has come from the ocean, to prevent him from leaving.
"My dear son, do not accept the invitation of Ulysses!
If you fight in the Trojan War, your glory will be eternal.
But you will never return.
If you stay here, glory will not be yours, but your life will be long."

Achilles, two destinies open before you. Which will you choose?

Achilles *must* go.
His heart tells him so.
An insult to honor cannot remain unpunished.
"We must go, Patroclus," he says to his friend,
boarding the black ship.

One morning, from the towers of Troy,
King Priam sees hundreds, thousands of black warships arrive.
They cover the sea.
King Priam sounds the alarm.
The women cry out. The children scatter.
The men race to their arms, to defend their city.

From his warship, King Agamemnon unleashes a fearful battle cry:
"Death to the Trojans!" He incites the Achaeans to disembark.
Achilles, Patroclus, Agamemnon, Ulysses. All go ashore.
And a host of warriors with them, too many to count.
All pursue the same dream:
destroy the wall of Troy and save the Achaean honor.
Become heroes and win eternal glory.

Fury is unleashed on the plains of Troy.
The two armies charge to attack.
Agamemnon, the king of kings, urges on his men.
Like a raging bull, the brave Achilles advances.
Patroclus, in shining armor, strikes left and right.

But the mighty walls of Troy hold fast.
Defending them is the great Hector, King Priam's son.
He leads an army of soldiers as brave as wild boars.
And so, year after year, the plains of Troy
ring with the sounds of weapons and war.

When the Achaean soldiers
are in need of food,
they sack the nearby cities.
They plunder gold, jewels,
and beautiful women.
Then they meet
to divide the spoils of war.
One day King Agamemnon is given
the lovely Chryseis as his slave.
Achilles receives Briseis.

The Achaeans do not know
that Chryseis is the daughter of Apollo's high priest.
They do not know that the god,
upon learning of the abduction,
resolves to unleash his wrath.
From high in the heavens he sends deadly arrows
on the Achaean camp.
For nine long days, without relief,
the soldiers are struck to the ground, one after another.

At last, on the tenth day,
the soothsayer Calchas speaks:
"Agamemnon, you must give back Chryseis.
Only thus can you placate Apollo's wrath."
But the king of kings protests:
"Why should I have to relinquish
my spoils of war?
Then I must receive another gift.
Achilles, I will take Briseis."

Anger and fear overtake Achilles:
"For whom do you think I came to fight?
For you I came,
to save your honor.
And now you repay me
by taking what I have deserved!
I will never fight again by your side,
never again!"
"Go your way then!" shouts back the king of kings.
"I don't need you!"

Agamemnon's soldiers
come to take away Briseis.
Achilles is forced to let her go.
But he loves her, even though she is his slave.
He loves her. And this love increases his wrath.
"You will regret this, Agamemnon!
Hector will kill you.
Hector will kill all the Achaeans.
Without me, you are lost."

Another thought devours him:
"It is a terrible thing
for a king to abuse his power
by taking away the belongings of another.
Why fight alongside
one who has no sense of honor?
I would like to say to all the Achaeans:
Return to your homes!
If there is no honor, nor glory,
then nothing is more precious than life."

Agamemnon's injustice is like a sharp knife
in Achilles's heart.
In front of the sea, he prays to his mother:
"I shall cease fighting, and I will never know glory,
but my life will be long,
as you told me the day of my departure.
Agamemnon has robbed me of my honor.
How can a man live without honor? How can I?
If only Zeus would intervene to restore it to me!"

And, behold, from the waters comes Thetis.
She has heard Achilles's words. She promises him:
"My son, I shall go to Zeus. I will implore him to make the Trojans victorious.
Agamemnon will realize his folly. And honor and glory will be yours."

Achilles, how will Zeus intervene
in order that you may fulfill your destiny?

With the help of Zeus, and without Achilles fighting against them,
the Trojans push forward to the enemy ships.
Just one more move, and Hector will burn the ships.
Agamemnon will be destroyed,
and with him the Achaean soldiers.

But Patroclus implores Achilles:
"Agamemnon asks your pardon.
He will cover you with riches if you return to fight.
I beg you, cast aside your anger and help us!
Or send me in your place. Let me wear your armor.
The Trojans will think that I am you, and they will run away."

"No, Patroclus," Achilles replies.
"I do not want Agamemnon's riches.
I have sworn that I will not fight, and so it must be.
Wear my armor. Go in my place."

Achilles, you asked Zeus to intervene.
Now the god is on the Trojan's side.
He will let Hector kill your brave friend.

When Achilles sees the lifeless body of Patroclus,
sorrow fills him from head to toe.
The great Achilles falls to the ground.
He crashes like a tree.
And lets out a fearful roar.

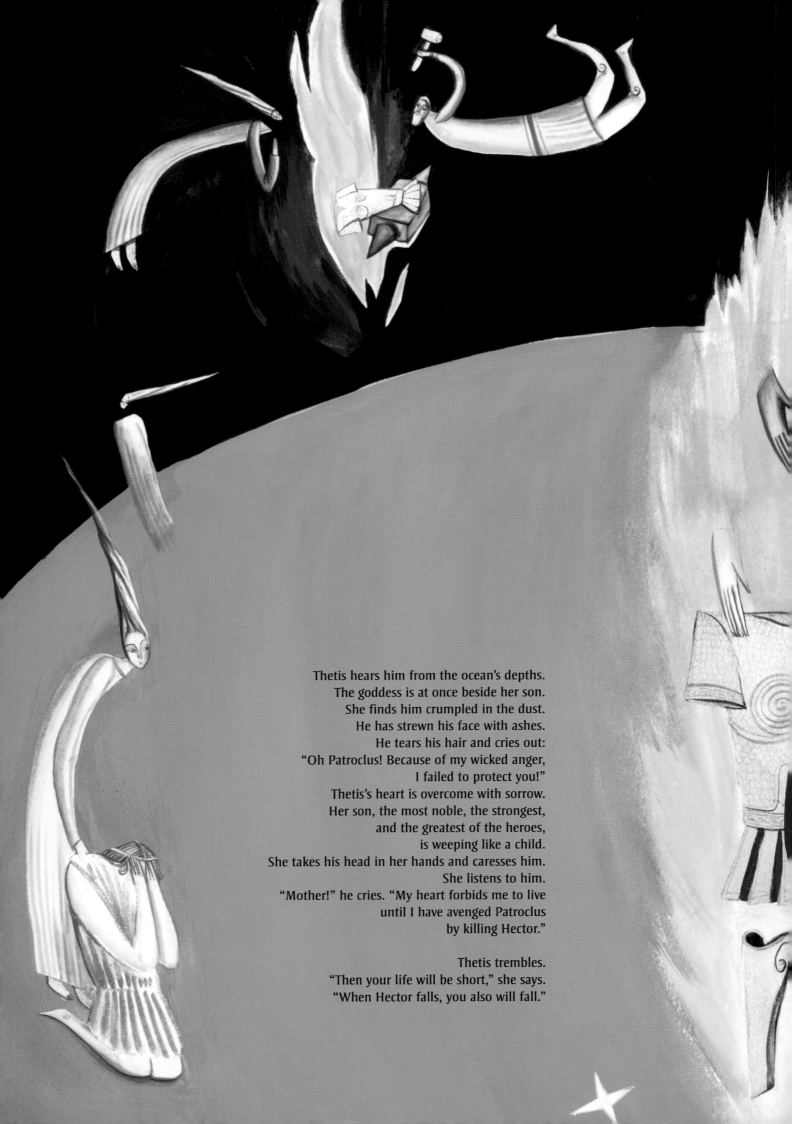

Thetis hears him from the ocean's depths.
The goddess is at once beside her son.
She finds him crumpled in the dust.
He has strewn his face with ashes.
He tears his hair and cries out:
"Oh Patroclus! Because of my wicked anger,
I failed to protect you!"
Thetis's heart is overcome with sorrow.
Her son, the most noble, the strongest,
and the greatest of the heroes,
is weeping like a child.
She takes his head in her hands and caresses him.
She listens to him.
"Mother!" he cries. "My heart forbids me to live
until I have avenged Patroclus
by killing Hector."

Thetis trembles.
"Then your life will be short," she says.
"When Hector falls, you also will fall."

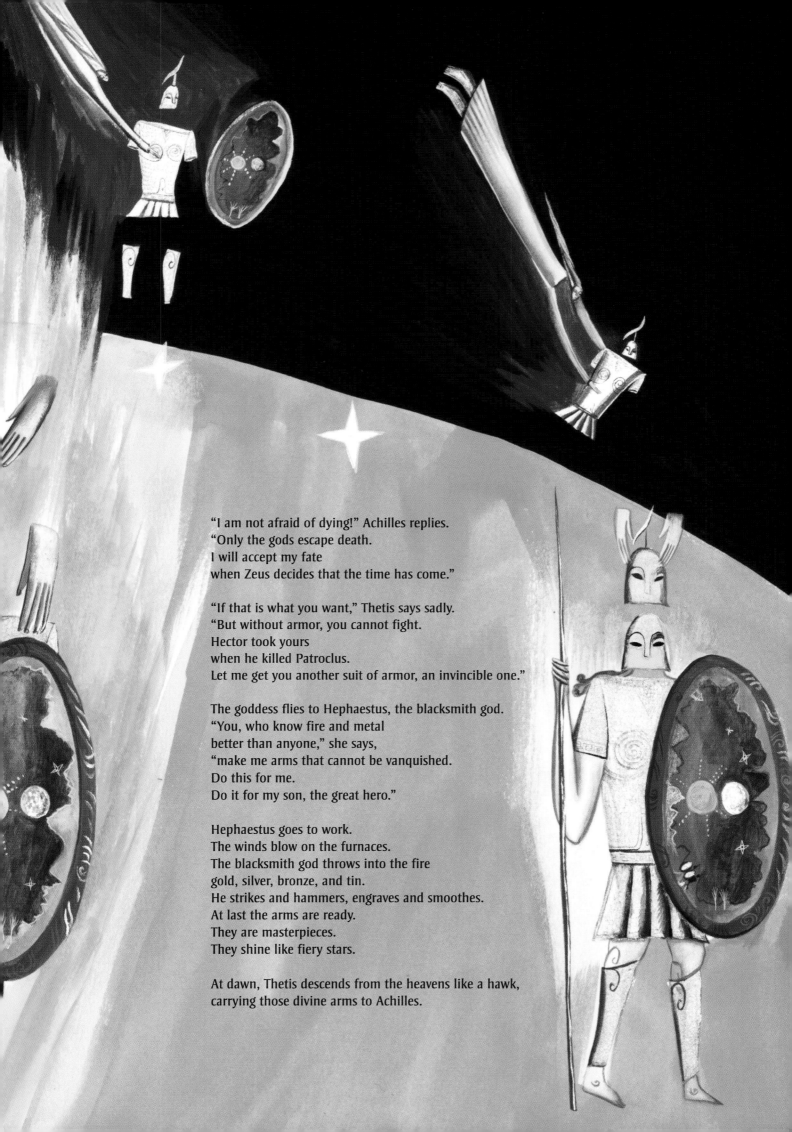

"I am not afraid of dying!" Achilles replies.
"Only the gods escape death.
I will accept my fate
when Zeus decides that the time has come."

"If that is what you want," Thetis says sadly.
"But without armor, you cannot fight.
Hector took yours
when he killed Patroclus.
Let me get you another suit of armor, an invincible one."

The goddess flies to Hephaestus, the blacksmith god.
"You, who know fire and metal
better than anyone," she says,
"make me arms that cannot be vanquished.
Do this for me.
Do it for my son, the great hero."

Hephaestus goes to work.
The winds blow on the furnaces.
The blacksmith god throws into the fire
gold, silver, bronze, and tin.
He strikes and hammers, engraves and smoothes.
At last the arms are ready.
They are masterpieces.
They shine like fiery stars.

At dawn, Thetis descends from the heavens like a hawk,
carrying those divine arms to Achilles.

Clad in immortal arms,
Achilles confronts the Trojans
and attacks on all sides.
To all he brings death and pain.
The river becomes a grave.
Trembling bodies seek refuge in the waters.
Lifeless bodies float by.

Finally the river, disgusted, protests:
"Stop, Achilles! Go far from me
to carry out this massacre!"
The river swells and foams.
It floods the plains of Troy.
It wishes to stop Achilles at all costs,
to drown him.

Then the gods intervene.
Zeus, Poseidon, and Athena.
They send Hephaestus to light his fires,
in order to dry up the river and calm it.
It is not Achilles's fate to die like this.

The river retreats.
Achilles, unstoppable, pursues the Trojans,
who flee in terror toward the city walls.

King Priam sees the Trojans running
and orders open the gates of Troy.
He lets them enter.
But his son Hector wishes to remain outside.
"I must defend my city!" Hector says.
Yet when he sees Achilles,
he is overtaken by terror
and runs away.
In a thundering voice Achilles shouts:
"Hector! Where is your courage?"
Hector stops at once.
It is his destiny that roots him to the spot.
He must face his destiny.

The tip of Achilles's spear shines like a star.
Hector falls lifeless to the ground.

But Achilles's anger is not calmed.
He ties Hector's body to his chariot
and orders the horses to set off at a gallop.
He drags Hector's body through the dust to the Achaean camp.

During the night, like a thief,
King Priam enters Achilles's tent.
Weeping, he kisses Achilles's hands,
the terrible hands that killed his son.
"Achilles," he says, "I beg of you.
Return to me Hector's body!
He died like a hero, defending his city.
But if I cannot bury him,
he will remain without honor."

Achilles studies the old man.
He watches the tears fall from the king's eyes.
He sees the grief on his face.
And Achilles is moved.
What difference is there
between the sorrow caused by Hector's death
and the sorrow caused by Patroclus's death?
There is no difference.
It is the same sorrow.

On that unbelievable night,
the two enemies embrace.
Achilles, the divine Achilles,
now feels that he is a man among men.

"King Priam," he says, "take your son."
"Hector was a great man. He died fulfilling his destiny.
Carry him home and bury him with the honor he deserves.
I promise you that I will hold back the army
and will not fight until the funeral rites are over."